When Henry "wakes up," he finds himself walking along an empty stretch of road on modern-day San Juan Island. He doesn't remember much about himself, besides his name and the fact that he's dead. How did he die? How long ago? What was his life? Did he have a family? Why is he still on the island? And most important, what is a ghost like him supposed to do now?

On Henry's journey of discovery, he meets another ghost in the same predicament—a little girl named Charlotte. Together they navigate the byways of the island and of their own memories, in search of the keys that will finally free them for departure.

Part ghost story, part historical novel, part fable, Anne L. Watson's latest offering weaves island lore, human insight, and spiritual wisdom into a magical tale of redemption and fulfillment.

Also by Anne L. Watson

Skeeter: A Cat Tale
Pacific Avenue
Joy
Flight
Cassie's Castaways
Willow's Crystal
Benecia's Mirror
A Chambered Nautilus

ANNE L. WATSON

DEPARTURE

Shepard & Piper
Friday Harbor, Washington

DEPARTURE

1

When I woke up, or came to, or whatever it was, I was walking south on Roche Harbor Road. South*ward*, anyway. That road turns and curves, and at any moment, you might be walking east or west, even if you are headed south in the end. That's the way San Juan Island is—a lot of hills, and the roads wind and twist. It's easy to end up in places you hadn't planned to go.

I didn't know how I knew all this, or how I knew my name was Henry, and that I was a middle-aged man—not a very good man or a very bad one. Or that I'd belonged here on the island when I was alive.

Or that I was dead.

It might have been a strange thing, knowing I was dead, but it wasn't any stranger than when I was alive and knew it. Just another fact.

What I didn't remember right away was *when* I'd lived, or whether I'd had a family, or why I died—most of the things you might think are important.

So I was a ghost with a lot to learn.

I checked to see if I was invisible. I should be, I thought. But I could see my own hand—it was muscular and callused. And scarred. An ugly hand, one that had worked hard and never been treated well.

But after a minute, I realized that seeing myself didn't prove much. I could still be invisible to living people.

Next thing I noticed was my clothes—a blue work shirt and denim overalls. Everything was clean, and the shirt was ironed, but I could tell it was old because the cuffs were fraying.

I had good strong boots on my feet, but one of the laces was almost worn through. I frowned. Not sure if it would break, or if I could get new ones if it did. I wished I'd kept up my clothes better when I was alive, but maybe I didn't have the money. That made sense to me: No, I had not had much money.

I was making progress, I thought. Getting some idea who I'd been. Poor. That's who I'd been.

The road surface was hard—much more solid than the old mud trough that

Roche Harbor Road used to be. I wondered what they'd done to it. It looked like
it would work pretty well, even in the rain.
But it wasn't easy on my feet.

I walked on, not knowing why. The
sun wasn't quite up yet, but the sky was
light and clear, and I could see brown
and yellow leaves on maple trees against a
background of tall firs. So it was autumn.
It looked like it was going to be the kind
of day when a man would be glad to be
alive. Only, of course, I wasn't.

A lot of things about the world were
coming back to me fast. Just in case
people could see me, I picked at some
loose threads on my shirt. I didn't want
to bring discredit to the spirit world with
my raggedness. Or get taken for a hobo, if

they mistook me for a live man. I pulled off one long thread and let the breeze blow it from my hand, wondering what would happen. As soon as it left me, it disappeared.

More of my life started to come to me, like a story, or maybe a dream. My life, and life on the island in general. Memories— a dead man's memories of some time past. Walking brought them back to me, like winding up an old clock that had been stopped for a while.

So, I recalled more and more as I put the road behind me. I was a rough man, a poor man. An unnoticeable man, even when I was alive. I thought I might have been a logger, or maybe a cannery worker or fisherman.

Out of nowhere, I recalled there'd been a lime works up at Roche Harbor, and I thought I might have worked there. I hoped not—it was a hard life, working the limekilns. But then, I wasn't an old man, and I was dead, so maybe that had been my lot. Whatever it was, I thought, I was free of it now.

I didn't have any strong feeling that anyone missed me now or grieved over me. Or maybe ever had. Could have been wrong about that, though—when I was alive, I might have been the kind of man who thinks no one gives a damn, even when they do. A woman must have ironed my shirt, and maybe she'd loved me. But it could be she'd passed on long ago, too.

I still had no idea how long it had been since I'd died.

It was just breaking dawn, and in the quiet of that early morning, I heard the motor car coming before I saw it. It sounded different from the ones I'd known. I didn't know if I ought to step out of the road, but I was already dead, so there didn't seem much point.

The headlights came on scary and blinding, even to a ghost. The car didn't brake, so that answered my question about whether anyone could see me. Probably, anyway.

It passed right through me, or I passed right through it. Inside, it was cold and soft and full of some kind of loud music out of nowhere. That was about all I could tell in the second or two before I was through.

I wasn't hurt, but I was a little shaken. I watched as it drove into the distance. It had red lights on the back, and it sure was moving fast. I guessed that motor cars had changed a lot since my time. And I began to think my time might be a ways back.

I plodded on for a while, but my feet started hurting more and more. That was the darnedest thing—that a ghost could get blisters and bruises. It didn't make sense. How could it be that a car could drive right through me without doing me any damage, but my boots could rub my feet raw?

There didn't seem to be any rules about being dead, and I minded that. And I was *surprised* to mind it, in a way that made me suspect I hadn't been much for rules when I was alive.

I recalled that ghosts were supposed to be able to fly and float. Or to just appear somewhere by thinking about a place and wishing to be there. I tried wishing first, because at least I knew how to do that. I put my whole mind to being down on Front Street. I could see the place like I was there, but it didn't get me any closer. Maybe wishing didn't work any better now than when I was alive.

Then I tried flying and floating, but it was a relief there was no one to see me, supposing they could have. I must have looked like a crazed chicken, and I felt like an awful fool. I didn't get anywhere doing that, either. It was like something was tying me to the earth or weighing me down.

So, I went on putting one foot in front of the other, and pretty soon, they quit hurting, and I was walking along again at a good pace, headed for town.

2

When I got to Friday Harbor, I could see one reason wishing might not have worked. The place I'd been picturing wasn't there anymore. I recognized a lot of buildings, but there was more that hit my eyes as unfamiliar—even though I still had no clear idea what had been there in my time, or exactly *when* my time had been.

But memories started to flood back as I looked around at the closed-for-the-night buildings. What came into focus as "mine" were the bank, the old drugstore, and bits of most of the shops. The bank didn't seem to be a bank anymore, and I felt glad about that—as if they'd somehow done me wrong when I was alive.

The boardwalks were gone, replaced by hard surface. The street was the same hard stuff as on Roche Harbor Road—not blocks like bricks but all one piece. Those were good changes—I remembered the mud, and how hard it was to go anywhere during rainy times. Not that I'd had much time or leisure to wander around. Or money for buying things.

I suddenly remembered the company store scrip up at Roche. I knew then for sure I'd worked the kilns up there.

I walked along the empty streets, looking at everything the way a foreigner might. It was hard to believe some of the things in the store windows—almost all

of them looked useless, and I was sure
some wouldn't have been shown like that
in my day. Some of the women's clothes on
display there—right on the main street—
made me look away. I wondered if ghosts
blushed. I tried to see my reflection in one
of the windows, but of course I had no
reflection. All I could see was the clothing on display, clothing that even harlots
wouldn't have worn in public when I was
alive.

That clinched it. I must have been dead
for quite a while. And *that* brought up
an uneasy kind of question: Where had I
been in the meantime?

That question brought churches to
mind, and how they'd preached about
the afterlife. I was sure I hadn't been

a churchgoing man, but I remembered church people, and how they talked about heaven and hell. They made going there sound like it was a trip to a real place like Olympia or Sacramento. Except there were only the two places you could go, one or the other.

I would have wound up in hell if they were right, but here I was, walking around, the same way I'd done when I was alive. And as far as I knew, hell wasn't like the county jail—it wasn't a sentence for a particular period of time, and then they let you go. So, I probably hadn't gone to hell after all.

No way I could have made it to that heaven they talked about, I was sure of that. Anyway, if you went to heaven, why would they send you back?

Like everything else, it didn't make sense.

But maybe the church people were wrong about there being only two places. If so, I might find other spirits like myself in town. I hadn't seen any, but I might not have found where they hung out yet.

Or maybe the church people were right, but something had misfired in my case. I wondered if my body and spirit had gotten stuck together somehow, and I'd been trapped in my grave till the last of my body was gone. Say my spirit was finally free, but God had forgotten about me by now, so I wasn't bound for anyplace. It could have been worse, I figured. I wouldn't call San Juan Island heaven, but it fell considerably short of hell.

If this was where I was slated to spend eternity, I was going to have to learn my way around. Figure out how to get what I needed—and I didn't even know yet what that might be. The rules for ghosts, if there were any, were confusing. If my feet could hurt, I might also feel hunger or cold. If I did need food or shelter, what would I do?

Of course, I must have had a house, or maybe a room, when I was alive. Must have been up at Roche. Most likely, none of those places were there anymore. If they were, someone else would live there now.

I'd have to find another place to stay. But it might not be a good idea to move into someone's house. I didn't want to scare anyone. That is, if people were even afraid of ghosts anymore, which I couldn't be sure about. Maybe *people* had changed, just like women's clothes. But that wasn't something to count on.

So, I couldn't plan on having a regular home. But there were lots of other buildings—shops here along Spring Street, some of them empty. The old courthouse was probably still there, too. At night, it would be an ideal place for a ghost. Might not be bad in the daytime, either. A dead man might fit in just fine over there.

But before I made plans, I needed to find out my limitations. And any advantages, too. I'd heard ghosts could pass through walls, so I walked casually at some glass doors, as if they were open.

I melted right through.

3

Inside was some kind of shop, but it was huge, and nothing at all was familiar. By then, I didn't expect things to be much like what I'd known, but even the feel of the inside was new. It wasn't like any place I'd been. Surely nothing like the company store at Roche.

Of course this was in town, where richer people would shop. Still, time had obviously made changes.

The first thing I saw was metal carts, all pushed together in crooked lines. I pulled one away from the others and tested it— it rolled pretty well. I took it to the back of the shop and looked it over. It didn't seem to be a toy, like a child's wagon. I didn't think they were for sale, either. Trying to stay out of sight of the front window, I rode the cart around, pushing with one foot to get going.

I quickly got tired of playing with it, so I explored more of the shop. The funny thing was, I could read all the packages, and I was pretty sure I'd never been able to read when I was alive. Of course, there were things I recognized, and many I didn't. I had no interest in eating, but I wondered if I *could* eat if I wanted to, so I tried to unwrap a piece of candy. I couldn't—my fingers went through the wrapper.

It surprised me that I could play with the cart but couldn't handle a piece of paper. Another bit of strangeness. I shrugged.

I probably wouldn't need to eat, anyway. Not now. More memories jostled one another—I'd known what it was to be hungry.

Losing interest in the shop, I tried to leave. But this time, I slammed into the doors as if I was real. Nothing worked to get me out of there—not wishing, or flying, or sidling. I kept hitting the glass like a stubborn bee.

Finally, I gave up and waited for the store to open, hoping I really was invisible. It didn't seem like there was *anything* I could count on.

When the place did open and customers started coming in, I was tempted to bolt for it. On second thought, I strolled out when someone opened the door, as if

I had every right to be there. If they saw me, I wouldn't attract attention. But it didn't seem that anyone did.

Out on the street, I was startled to see how many more people were dressed like workingmen—like me—than in my time. Overalls and waist overalls, work shirts and old coats. There were more women wearing trousers than I remembered, too. More memories—of a war, and women doing jobs that men used to. Wearing men's clothes because they had to. And then, no more memories. Maybe I'd died in the war, or soon after.

I went down to the harbor, which was only a couple of blocks from the big shop. A little girl was sitting on a bench there, crying, and I knew she was a ghost, too.

4

She was a pretty little thing, maybe ten years old. She had on a fancy pink party dress, ribbons in her curly yellow hair, shiny black shoes. She looked like one of the rich children from my time. Or maybe a while later, I thought, studying her. She was like children I'd seen, but just a touch different.

Of course, I'd never have spoken to a rich man's little girl when I was alive. But now that we were both dead, why not? So, I went to her and knelt on the ground.

"What's the matter?" I asked.

She sobbed. "I want my mother."

I sighed. I didn't really think I could help, but it tugged at me. I was sure I hadn't had children, but somehow, a little girl crying for her mother was something I couldn't ignore. "Where is she?"

"I don't *know*!" she wailed.

"We could look for her," I suggested. "But I don't think she's around here. At least, I haven't seen any women likely to be her."

I wanted to ask if her mother was dead. Or if she realized that *she* was. I thought she probably knew, but it didn't seem polite to ask. I guess children don't worry so much about that kind of thing, because the next words out of her mouth were, "You're a ghost."

I nodded. "So are you."

She didn't pipe up and agree with me, but she didn't disagree, either. "Where are the others?" she asked.

"Which others?"

"The other ghosts. We can't be the only ones."

It was a good question. I didn't know the answer.

"I haven't seen anyone. Just live people. I don't think they can see us."

"Where should we go?" she asked. "To find Mother, I mean."

I thought about it. "Maybe out to the cemetery? There might be more like us there."

She looked me over carefully. "Mother told me to not go with strange men."

"I'm not a man. Like you said, I'm a ghost."

She looked at me even more doubtfully. "She didn't say anything about that."

"Well, she wouldn't, would she," I said. "Look, it's all right. The rules are different now. Or maybe there aren't any. I'm Henry. What's your name?"

"Charlotte."

"That's a pretty name. Charlotte. Where was your house when you were alive? We could go there."

"I don't know."

She looked like she was about to cry again, so I said, "You know, if we walk out toward the cemetery, we might meet your mother on the way. Or maybe she'll be out there, or someone else you know. We can try."

She scrubbed her hand across her face, erasing the tears. She nodded without saying any more, and we both stood up. It was a long way from the harbor to the cemetery, but I didn't think that was likely to matter.

The town was awake now, the streets thronged with people, but we passed by everyone unseen. We walked along quietly together, and after a while, Charlotte slipped her hand into mine.

No child had ever held my hand before. I was sure of it. I couldn't possibly have forgotten how it felt to be trusted like that.

5

The cemetery was out of town, a couple of miles from the harbor. We walked along, staying at the side of the road, even though I knew there wasn't any reason to avoid the motor cars. For a while, Charlotte stared at them, frightened, so I could tell she hadn't seen anything quite like them when she was alive. There must have been cars in her time if *I* remembered them, but these were sleek and fast.

"It's different now," I said. "Looks like everything's faster."

She nodded, staying close to me as another whizzed by.

"We can't get hurt anymore," I said. "It's not the same as when we were alive."

"How do you know?"

"One went right through me this morning. Or I went right through it. Anyway, it didn't hurt."

But we kept away from them, not yet ready to give up the ways of living people. We trudged along the edge of the road, right on the lip of a ditch filled with blackberries. That was familiar, anyway. The children used to gather them in the wild places, used to bring them home in pails for their mothers to make pies. Free food, even if the berries might be small and seedy. Mattie would've . . .

Mattie? Was that the woman who'd ironed my shirt? Did she make pies from the island berries? Was her name Martha, or maybe Matilda?

———

A pair of skilled, chapped hands. A woman's hands. Rolling dough, sprinkling a little flour to make it come out right. Henry was right on the edge of saying something to the woman, something important—then he couldn't find the words.

———

"How much farther is it?" Charlotte asked.

"Why? Do your feet hurt?"

"No, but it's not any fun to just walk and walk."

"We could talk more, to pass the time. Do you remember anything about your life?"

She thought for a while. I noticed yellow flowers as we walked along. Weeds along the road. A few leaves blowing. A yellow bird clinging to the stem of a thorny plant. Maybe it saw us, maybe it didn't. The day was peaceful. There was nothing left to want.

"I had a mother and father," she said, finally.

"When was your time?" I asked.

"I don't know. Maybe I'll remember later?"

"Don't let it worry you. It's not easy to call back." And harder for a kid, I figured.

"When was yours?"

"I think it must have been around the time they had the Great War, but I wasn't a soldier."

"I went to school. I remember that."

So far, she could have been almost any child. But for all I knew about myself, I could have been almost any workingman, too. Death had turned us into anybodies.

"Is Mother dead, too?"

"I don't know. If she's not, I don't reckon we'll see her at the cemetery, unless she's visiting your grave."

"Why are we going there, then?"

"She might be there," I said patiently. "Or if she isn't, there might be someone there who knows something. We probably shouldn't be here on the island, you know. We ought to be in heaven." I had almost added "or hell," but I wasn't going to scare a little girl like that.

"Why aren't we?"

"I don't know."

The road curved, the way roads do, and there was a crossroads all of a sudden, with a little store at the corner. The sign out front said Antiques.

"What are antiques?" I asked Charlotte. "Do you know?"

"Old stuff. Mother used to like places like this. They're boring."

"Oh." I shrugged. It did sound boring. "We might as well go on, then."

"Let's go in," she said.

"You want to? Why?"

"I just want to see. Just for a minute."

I wondered if she hoped to find her mother in there. I didn't think it was likely. But we had plenty of time.

"Wait," I said. "Let's watch first. Get an idea what it's like."

We stood in the shade of roadside trees.
A car pulled up in front of the store, and
the couple in it got out. They both wore
waist overalls like miners, and some kind
of loose coats or jackets. I was glad the
woman wasn't wearing the kind of clothes
in the Spring Street windows, but then,
I guessed it wasn't warm enough. Maybe
they wore things like that at home.

When they'd gone inside, I walked
slowly over to the car, trying to take in
all the details. It was like the one I'd passed
through, very different from the ones I
remembered from my time. For one thing,
it was red. Lower and smoother, less like a
carriage. More like a boat, or even a sled.

I passed through the car door into the
front seat, wondering if I could drive it.

I had never driven a car before, as far as I could remember. I wasn't even sure I'd ridden a horse.

Charlotte appeared on the seat beside me. "What are you doing?"

"I thought I might try driving."

"You're going to *steal* a car?"

"I doubt I could. I don't know how to make it work. Besides, what would I do with a car? People would see it."

I gave up, though the idea of driving the rest of the way to the cemetery was appealing.

We drifted out of the car, and I noticed that the back of it had a license plate— I remembered those. At the top were two small, shiny rectangles. One said APR, the other said 2009.

If that was the date, or close to it, I must have been dead a long, long time.

6

It was dim inside the store. Only two customers, the couple we saw go in. They were looking at a rocking chair, rocking it back and forth, checking the finish, deciding whether to buy it. Charlotte was right—it looked old. I remembered chairs like that from porches in front of rich people's houses, but of course, theirs were new. I couldn't imagine why people who could own that red car—which I figured they did—would want to buy a beat-up old piece of furniture.

"Your mother used to buy things like that?" I asked Charlotte.

"Oh, yes. Mostly older than that. She liked antiques. That chair doesn't look very old."

"Were you poor?"

She laughed. "Of course not. Daddy owned a store."

"But only poor people buy old things."

"Antiques are different, Henry. Don't you know that?"

She gave me a scornful look, the way a rich lady would have looked at a dumb mill hand in my day. It reminded me that, even if we were both dead now, we were completely different classes. My anger surprised me—I would have thought a ghost would be beyond all that. But it came from somewhere so far inside that I knew it had been a big part of my life.

I sighed, reminding myself that Charlotte was just a kid. And whatever we were doing here—whether the heaven and hell stuff was right or not—it really did seem time to rise above how I used to be.

Angry, I thought. Yes, I'd been angry. When I was alive, I'd seen the clean people who wore pretty clothes and led easy lives. Seen the yachts docked in the harbor up at Roche. Seen the owner of the lime works, Mr. McMillin, and his family. And I'd kept on sweating and straining, stoking the fires that slaked the lime that made their fortune. Gone on being paid in scrip you could only use at their company store.

Wouldn't anyone have been angry at all that?

Now, though, I wished I could stop, and I meant it. But wishing wasn't going to do it, not right away.

I looked around for Charlotte. She was almost at the back of the store, staring at some pictures on the wall.

I headed in her direction, studying the merchandise as I went. It all looked old and used, but the prices were unbelievable. I spent some time looking over old cook-ware and laundry tools. When I touched a cracked wooden washboard, I suddenly thought of Mattie again—could see her as if she was there. She came clearer and clearer, her sweet face looking at me puz-zled-like, the way she did when I was in a mood.

The memories tumbled over one another, faster and faster. I saw her making
biscuits like she used to, shelling peas,
washing clothes. Always, always, washing clothes and ironing them. That was
how she made her living—with her washboard and her sad irons in the fire. I didn't
know anymore why she'd had to, but that
was who she was when I knew her, the
laundress for the factory. Or one of them,
anyway.

For a few seconds, she was so real.
I saw her look up, tired but still smiling,
and brush a strand of curly brown hair off
her forehead with the back of her hand.
I touched my blue shirt to thank her for
all the things she'd done for me, and she
disappeared again into the past.

At the back of the store, Charlotte looked almost like she was falling into one of the pictures. I hurried back to see what she'd found.

It was an ordinary-looking thing, the picture. Photograph, really. Wood frame, glass over it. I'd never owned things like that, of course, but I'd seen them often enough.

This one showed a line of well-dressed women—some rich ladies' organization, probably. They'd had them in my day. Another thing that had riled me—Mattie having to work so hard to make women like these look pretty. Like they were the only ones who mattered, while she wore faded old clothes that couldn't be ruined by hard work.

Charlotte pointed to one of the women. "She's a friend of Mother's."

A card on the wall next to the frame gave a date of 1935. If that was Charlotte's time, and if the number on the license plate outside was this year, her mother and everyone else she knew were surely dead and gone.

Charlotte's eyes were full of tears, and I knew I didn't have to tell her. She knew. I felt sorry for her. It was one thing for a grown man to be dead, but it wasn't fair for a kid like her to have never had a life. For the first time, I wondered why she'd died, what had happened.

My leftover anger dimmed and went out like a lamp that had run out of oil. Sure, she was a rich man's kid—well, rich compared to me, anyway. That didn't put her on McMillin's level, but her parents probably wouldn't even have looked at a workingman. Just the same, both of us were dead now—what difference could any of that make?

"Let's head over to the cemetery," I said, "and see if we can find anyone."

I knew I wouldn't find Mattie, though. She wouldn't have a grave with a stone, all carved with her name and her dates of birth and death. No epitaph saying who'd loved her, or that she was in the arms of Jesus, or anything.

I felt the anger flare again, thinking of Mattie, my Mattie, in some potter's field. I pushed it back, determined not to carry it with me anymore. Whatever had been wrong in my time—and I knew there was plenty—it was over and done. I had to keep reminding myself of that.

7

I took Charlotte's hand again, and we left the store. I gave the car just one backward glance. I would have loved to drive it, or even catch a ride. At least it had told me what year it was. That was good to know, though it left me wondering all over again where I'd been and what I'd been doing since the time I probably died. Almost a century is a long time.

As we walked down the road, I was trying to think two things at once. One was that how I'd been seeing things lately wasn't much like the old Henry. When I was alive, I'd never have thought twice about minding the way a rich girl spoke to me.

I wouldn't have hurt anyone—child or grown-up—but I'd have stoked my anger like a kiln fire, brooding over it a long time. As I had, probably all my life, about being poor. I was having ideas now that I'd never had before. Seeing things a new way.

So, maybe there was more to the afterlife than heaven and hell. Maybe this was a kind of school. It could be I wasn't really on San Juan Island at all, I just thought I was. What could a man like me know about the afterlife? I'd never had much schooling, or maybe none, and I hadn't gone to church. Tried to figure things out on my own, the best I could. Probably hadn't made a very good job of it.

The other thing on my mind was Mattie. I knew I'd wanted to marry her, but somehow I didn't think I had. Maybe I'd decided I was too poor to support a wife, or maybe she'd refused me. The way I'd seen her, just for a few seconds, back in the store made me long to see her again. To remember everything about her—the way she walked, the turn of her head, the sound of her voice.

Mattie, Mattie . . .

———

Henry stood watching while Mattie pegged out clothes—the good clothes of managers and their wives, the ragged overalls and shirts of the workingmen. She handled them all the same—as if they were precious. She washed bedsheets, too, and other linens. Anything they handed her, she made it clean, and dried it in the sun when it shone, and smoothed it with her sad irons.

When there was no sunshine, Mattie and the other laundresses hung the clothes indoors. It made a damp, miserable mess, but she never complained. Henry sometimes wondered what she had to smile about, the way she smiled. Like she knew a wonderful secret that maybe, someday, she'd tell him.

Henry wanted her the way men want women, but he didn't like to think about that. Because he wanted other women too, sometimes, or wanted what he did with them in the brothels at the edge of town. He didn't have enough money to go there often, but he'd had loose women like that. And now he didn't want to think about those times either, because he wanted Mattie in the same way, but it wasn't right. Not a good woman like Mattie.

———

"How far is it to the cemetery?"

I shook my head to clear it, and my longing for Mattie drifted away. Charlotte was looking up at me, waiting for an answer. I thought maybe she hadn't been taken to visit the cemetery, she was so young. Or maybe she had, and she'd forgotten.

"I don't think it's a lot farther now," I said.

I'd wondered whether I was blushing, back on Spring Street, looking at the clothes women wore in this time. But I knew I was now. I could feel my face getting hot for even thinking about those women at the edge of town, here with a little girl right beside me, and a rich man's daughter at that.

I'd never been a very good man, and I guessed I still wasn't.

8

When we got to the cemetery, a man and an old woman were standing together at the entrance, near the little church. Since they couldn't see us anyway, we stopped to listen to them.

"I don't think he'll hurt anything," the woman said. "Really, Tom, I don't see what he *could* hurt."

The man frowned. "We can't let a homeless man stay in the cemetery. He could desecrate the graves."

"I don't see how, since he doesn't seem to have tools or paint."

"He could piss on them."

She looked amused. "Do you think that what goes on in a grave could be any uglier, objectively, than it already is?"

He ignored her question. "Or even worse. He could shit on Dad's grave."

"The birds and foxes have probably been doing that for years. And if he does, it's really the groundskeeper's problem, not ours."

"You honestly don't care?"

"Your *dad* probably wouldn't have cared. For a biologist, that's all just part of the cycle of nature. Very little shocked him. In fact, if I remember correctly, *nothing* did—except unkindness."

Her comment was clearly a reproof for her son. He looked furious, but said nothing. I tugged on Charlotte's hand,

and we moved away. Looking back, I saw the man and woman get into separate cars and drive off.

"What's homeless?" Charlotte asked.

"Maybe she means a hobo," I said. "I guess they don't have homes."

"What's a hobo?"

I didn't know what they'd been called in her time, but they must have existed. Maybe she'd been sheltered by her parents so she wouldn't see the ugly side of life.

"Some people are really poor," I said. "They can't find work and they have no place to go."

"Where do they sleep?"

"Anywhere they can. In the woods, or any quiet place. Like here."

"What do they eat?"

"Whatever they can get, I guess."

"Were you a hobo, Henry?"

"No," I said, trying my best to act better than the hothead I'd been when I was alive. "I was a workingman, up at Roche Harbor at the lime works."

She frowned. "Daddy said they were rough men."

I stopped walking and she looked up at me, still holding my hand. "Did any of the men up at the lime works ever hurt you?" I asked.

"No."

"Did any of them ever hurt anyone you knew?"

"I don't think so."

"Then do you think your father might have been mistaken?"

She was quiet for a moment. "Maybe so," she said, and a shadow I didn't understand passed across her face. Kids that age shouldn't have big troubles—but they do. Even rich kids, pretty little girls in frilly pink dresses.

For sure, Charlotte had had at least one trouble big enough to die from. Because here she was in 2009, holding hands with another ghost and searching through a cemetery to try to find out what had happened to her.

9

It wasn't hard to find the hobo—or homeless man, as they seemed to be called now. It wasn't that large a cemetery to begin with. But also, he was the kind of guy who just got noticed, for some reason.

He was sitting on the ground between two graves, not doing anything disrespectful—but I saw what the old lady's son had meant. The man's hair was long and dirty, and his clothes were rags. He hadn't shaved in years, probably. He looked seedy and rough, like someone who might do something bad, even if he hadn't yet.

I cringed at my thoughts. Weren't they the same as what Charlotte thought about me? Didn't it make me mad when she said things like that? Why was it any better for *me* to judge a man for his looks than it was for her?

But I thought, it *was* different. If I'd been alone, I probably wouldn't have worried about it. I might have expected the worst of the fellow, but I could always take care of myself. Charlotte made it different. She was just a little girl, even if she did act like a snobbish lady sometimes. Her mother had told her not to trust strange men, and here we were looking for her mother. And if this homeless man wasn't strange, no man ever was.

On the other hand, how could anybody hurt her now? I was having a hard time getting it through my head that Charlotte was *dead*. Wasn't any trouble at all to think that about myself—it seemed natural. But I wanted something better for Charlotte. A little girl in a frilly party dress was supposed to have a good life ahead of her. What kind of careless God would let something bad happen to a girl in a pink dress?

Anyway, I didn't trust the homeless man. I was starting to pull her away when he looked up at us.

"Don't worry," he said.

I was astonished he spoke to us. "You can see us!"

"Oh, yes."

"Are you dead?"

"No," he said, "I'm not."

"No one else can see us."

He smiled. "You'll find that a few people can. It depends."

I wasn't sure what it might depend on,
and I wasn't sure I wanted to know. So I
just said, "Oh," and left it at that.

He just looked quietly at us, still smiling a little.

"We're looking for Charlotte's mother,"
I said.

He shrugged slightly. "There's no one
here but me."

The way he said that really spooked
me, and I turned away, still pulling on
Charlotte's hand. We could probably find
her mother's grave if we looked around.
Supposing she'd died here, and been buried here. Supposing that was what the
family wanted. I didn't really know how

people did those things—and it suddenly occurred to me, when it came to family, I'd almost never had one.

———

Everything had happened so fast. It was one afternoon—he didn't remember anything special about that morning. He came in for dinner, came in from the street where he'd been playing with the other boys. A man blocked the stairs, wouldn't let him go to his mother. Henry had seen him only a couple of times before.

"Kid, I'm sorry. Your mother's dead."

Henry didn't understand. He knew about dead animals—bugs, rats. There were enough of them *in the rooming house. Mostly alive, but he knew what dead was—the rats mangled in traps, the beetles squashed underfoot.*

But Mother was a person. People couldn't be dead.

He tried to go up to their room. The man grabbed his arm.

"You can't go there now," he said. "I'll take you to the old lady."

The "old lady" lived in the room where Mother went to pay the rent. Or to ask for more time. She looked at Henry like he was one of those bugs or rats. He shivered.

"You can't stay here," she said, looking away from him. "I'll send round to the home."

Home? What home? This was home. But two women came and took him to a big building. Big and cold.

He cried. Almost all the time. They tried to get him to stop, but he couldn't.

"You won't find another family if you keep on like that."

He didn't want another family. He wanted his mother. He cried more. Finally, they put him on a big train with other children.

"You'll go to a good home out West," a lady said. She was the one on the train who gave them food. He tried to smile at her, but he couldn't stop the tears.

So, he just made himself as small as he could in the corner of the hard train seat. He was cold and scared. At night, it was so dark, he wondered if he was still alive.

On the second day, they stopped at a town. "Get out now," the food lady told the children. "People from your new homes will be here."

They sat on benches in the station waiting room. Men and women came and looked at them, talked about how strong they might be, how much farm work they might do. Henry sat at the end of a bench and cried without stopping. Nobody chose him.

The children who weren't chosen got back on the train. They stopped again at the next town, and the next. Finally, Henry was the only one left.

They were about to turn the train around and take Henry back to the big building, the Home, when a man and a woman hurried up to the platform.

"Is this all that's left?" the man asked. He looked down at Henry with a mean face.

"He's a fine, healthy boy," the food lady said. Henry cried.

"He's a crybaby," the man said. "Emma, I told you this wouldn't be any good."

The man's wife stooped to look in Henry's face. "What's your name, son?" she asked.

"Henry."

"How old are you, then?"

"I don't know."

"He's an idiot," the man said. "Emma, come away. This is useless."

"He's six years old," the food lady said. "He's upset now. He's not an idiot."

"He's a baby for six," the man said. "We want a boy who can work."

"Husband, if we'd had a son of our own, you'd have been pleased enough to think of him as a helper someday, even though he was just born. As I see it, this boy is six years ahead of what you would have expected. If we had a child of our own." Her voice cracked, sad and pleading.

The man sighed loudly. "Emma, I suppose you must have your way."

They signed the papers, and the man hoisted Henry into the back of their wagon. He cried all the way to their farm.

————

The homeless man called after us. "Look in the old part of the cemetery."

We walked around for a while, trying to find that part. He might have said to go right or left, or into the far corner, or something helpful. But he hadn't, and I wasn't going back to ask. Anyway, we found it on our own.

As we wandered among the graves, looking at the old stones, Charlotte cried out and pointed at one. She'd never told me her mother's name, but I guessed it must be her headstone. Especially since there were two names on it, and one of them was Charlotte's.

She and her mother had died the same day, back in August of 1931. There was nothing on the stone to say why.

"But where is Daddy buried?" she asked, looking at the tombstones to the right and left of her grave. Different names, no connection.

"Maybe he left the island after you died?"

She looked doubtful. "He had the store," she said. "I don't see how he could have left."

"He might have sold it."

"Maybe." She looked uneasy and confused. "But where's Mother now?"

"Not here anymore," I said. "She must be in heaven." It felt strange to say that, because I'd never believed in heaven. But if *we* weren't dead, everyone *else* must still be around . . . somewhere. I had no idea where, but it wouldn't hurt if Charlotte thought her mother was in a good and happy place.

"Where's *your* grave, Henry?"

That surprised me. "Up at Roche, if it's anywhere. But there won't be a marker."

"Why?"

"Like I told you, Charlotte, I was a poor man. Graves with stones aren't for poor people."

She frowned. "But you don't *know*."

"No, I don't."

"We could go look."

I sighed. "Might as well. We seem to have lots of time. Maybe forever. And maybe there'll be other things to see there."

As we left the cemetery, we passed by the homeless man again.

"Did you find the grave?" he asked.

"Yes, but her mother wasn't there now."

"No," he said. "I told you. No one's here but me."

His dirty hand rubbed across his eyes as if he was wiping away tears. But to me, it looked like an act. Or else like he was crazy.

Whichever, the man was spooky. I didn't trust him at all.

10

Time was passing in a way that seemed different from the ordinary. I could have sworn we'd spent less than a day getting around, since I didn't remember sleeping. But as we walked toward Roche Harbor, I could see winter coming fast. The leaves were all down from the trees, and they blew along the roadside like they were running away.

Maybe we *didn't* have forever.

————

Henry watched smoke curl up from the stubble fires after the harvest. Animals would run from it, frightened. He didn't like to watch that. He had nightmares in the fall about burning, animals burning, people burning.

"Still a lot of work to do," said his stepfather.

"A lot for you, Pa. I'm leaving."

"What'ya mean, leaving? You can't go with all this work here!"

"Do it yourself. Lincoln freed the slaves."

The old man drew himself back and glared at his eighteen-year-old stepson. "The dirt ain't even sunk good on Emma's grave, and already you think you don't owe us nothin'."

"Leave Ma Emma out of it. She was decent to me. You never were."

"I tried to make a man out of you, and she kept you a baby. She spoiled you, that's what it is. You were a sniveling baby when we found you, and you're still one. But I'll teach you yet."

The old man lunged. Henry knocked him down with one punch and ran. Glancing behind to see if his stepfather was coming after him, he almost stopped. The old man lay still on the ground, like a pile of trash. Henry hoped he wasn't dead. If he was, the sheriff would be sure to hunt down his killer.

———

"It's raining," said Charlotte.

It was. First a rattle of drops on the leaves, then it stopped. Then came back twice as hard. The raindrops fell right through us.

Charlotte extended her hands. "We're not getting wet!"

She jumped in a puddle, but it didn't splash. We both got silly then, running and jumping through the rain. We didn't get wet, or even breathless. We danced and jumped, and tried to spatter each other, laughing as our hands and feet went right through puddles.

Finally we stopped. Charlotte looked at me with a smile that was almost sly. I figured she'd never seen a grown man behave that way. For that matter, I hadn't either. And I couldn't much remember playing even when I was a child.

We dropped back to a walk, heading northward. Our silliness had passed quickly, and the clouds seemed to draw in and weigh us down.

"Are we going to look for your grave up there, or what?" Charlotte asked.

"I told you," I said. "There won't be a marker for me or any of my friends."

"Then what are we going to find?"

"I don't know. I just want to see where I lived. Just to see the place, just to be there another time."

"Who were your friends? What was it like when you were alive?"

"I don't remember so much, Charlotte. There was a woman I wanted to marry. I don't think I did, but I don't know why. Maybe I would have, if I hadn't died."

"When did you die, then?"

"It was right after the War, I think. I don't remember dying."

"I don't, either. My grandfather died after the war. It was before I was born. Mother told me there was bad sickness then, and a lot of people died."

A memory flashed into my mind— sick men in a bunkhouse. Coughing till they bled, groaning, crying for help. Blue lips, blue skin. I pushed it away in horror. I didn't want to know.

"Maybe that's when it was, Charlotte. I don't think we need to know the details. But I wish I knew why we're still here. Can't be too many people stuck like this, or we'd see them all over the place."

"Do you think we'll ever be able to leave?"

I wanted to give her a comforting answer, but I told the truth. "I hope so, but I don't know. Maybe we're stuck here for good."

"Tell me about your time." She seemed seriously interested now. I thought, even if she was dead, she was growing up.

"It was hard," I said. "I worked all the time, stoking the fires for the kilns—"

"What's stoking?"

"Adding wood so it'll keep burning and keep the rock at the right temperature."

I didn't think she wanted a lesson in lime production, and she didn't. "But you had to work all the time?"

"Pretty much. I'm not sure I can even say how hard it was."

Did "hard" cover the way Billy died? Did any word? Sure, he had to know dynamiting was the worst job in the place. One good thing, he probably never knew what hit him. I never looked for his grave, up there on the hill where they buried the dead from the works. Never even knew if he had one. Dynamiters, sometimes they didn't find enough to bury.

He'd been my friend. I don't know. Women could cry, men were supposed to go on with their jobs like it didn't happen. But I lay awake in the bunkhouse all that night. I never made a noise, but the tears ran down the side of my face and soaked into the bed.

Must have been the next day, I saw McMillin and some men, dressed in suits. Doing the tour of the kilns, I guess. Him showing off what a big guy he was. I wanted to knock him down like I did with Pa, knock them *all* down, and run away again. But I was on an island. I'd never have gotten away with it. And I had nowhere else to go, anyway.

"Did you make a lot of money?" Charlotte asked. "Daddy always said he worked hard to make money for us."

"Just scraped by, and they paid in scrip, so the only place I could spend it was the company store."

"What's scrip? What's a company store?"

"The company you work for pays you in coupons instead of money. The coupons are only good at a store they own, so you have to shop there. We could ask for money, but we didn't get as much if we did."

She looked at me in astonishment. "That's not fair!"

"No."

"Why did you work there?"

"Only job I could get. Or the only *kind* I could get."

"Why?"

I thought about the bits I'd remembered of my life. Finally I said, "I guess things went hard for me all along the way. It's just the way it worked out. But life up there at Roche was no picnic, that's for sure."

"But you told me my father was wrong when he said the workmen were rough!"

I thought about that too. "Some of them were. Some weren't. I'll tell you something I don't think I've ever told anyone, Charlotte. When I was young, I hit a man. He fell down and I ran away. I was afraid I'd killed him. For a long time, I was afraid they'd come and get me, put me in prison, maybe even hang me. I dreamed about it for years, dreamed I heard men with bloodhounds coming for me. They never did, but I never hit anyone else as long as I lived."

"But some of the men up there *were* bad?"

"There's good and bad everywhere. And there's different *kinds* of good and bad. To my mind, the worst ones at Roche were the bosses. They lived like kings, brought guests in on yachts, really rubbed our noses in how rich they were. When I think about it, I still feel raw."

"Maybe it's better not to think about it, then. I'm sorry I asked, Henry."

I glanced at her, startled. She still looked like a little girl, but she sounded more and more like a grown woman. Like she was making up for the time after she'd died. I hoped she wouldn't get old on me.

Then, too, I wondered if I was aging as well. Probably I was, but it would be harder to tell with a man in his fifties than with a child.

I'd thought we were trapped in an endless forever, always the same, almost as if there were no time at all. Now I realized it wasn't that way. How long had it been since Charlotte and I met? It seemed like less than a day, but weeks or even months had slipped by without me noticing—judging by how fast the season had changed. It could have even been years, if I thought about our own changes.

I'd worried about shelter at first, but I no longer thought we'd need that. I'd worried about food, but neither of us seemed to get hungry. Now I thought more about time. If we were aging, did that mean we'd get old? Did it mean we'd die again? Was that the only way for us to leave the island? How much time did we have left? What would happen to us next?

As if in answer, dark clouds began to spit snow at us.

"Come on," I said, pulling Charlotte by the hand. "We have to get up to Roche. It's getting late."

"But you said we had lots of time," she protested.

"I'm starting to think I was wrong. I've been wrong about a lot of things. Let's try flying. I couldn't do it before, but now I think we might."

We took off like two birds, and the island spread out beneath us like a map.

We headed straight for Roche, so I could
take my one last look.

11

It must have been an ordinary winter day in the real world, because people were walking around the streets at Roche Harbor, going about their business. The lime works was gone—nothing left but ruins of old kilns. There were signs everywhere about the history of the place, so people would know what it had been. But that so-called history wasn't everything I remembered.

In place of the old factory were sleek shops. The harbor where we'd loaded lime onto ships was packed with pleasure boats, descendants of McMillin's friends' yachts. It was all so different, I would have thought I'd never seen it before, if not for flashes of memory triggered by the outline of the harbor and the islands beyond.

The old company store—or what had replaced it—proudly showed "Roche Harbor Lime & Cement Co." on its side and "Company Store" over the door. But it was nothing like before—it was an ordinary market with a hardware sideline. We went in and looked around awhile, but just being there made me remember the old anger and hopelessness more than I could stand. Feeling like I was about to boil over, I hurried out, with Charlotte at my heels. I could see she was startled and confused by the change in me.

We wandered around the tiny town, but I recognized almost nothing. Maybe my memory of the place was finally going.

Maybe it had really changed that much. But I still had a feeling I needed to do something there, and I simmered with frustration.

Finally, we saw a sign pointing to the cemetery, and we headed that way. I was sure I'd never find the place I was buried, or Mattie either, but for sure, McMillin's grave would be there. The anger I'd had to bottle up all those years blazed out like I was stoking it with wood full of pitch pockets. Let it burn too hot—there was no foreman on my back now. McMillin was finally going to listen to my side— all I'd suffered, all I thought.

At first we saw only small graves. But beyond that, we came to what looked like a temple—a circle of columns topped by a ring, open to the sky. This had to be him—it was the showiest place around. I pounded up the three flights of steps that led to it.

Inside the circle, concrete chairs were set around a concrete table. A sign said the chairs contained the ashes of the McMillins, who had believed they'd sit there feasting through eternity—or something like that. It would be just like the old man, I thought, to sit on a hill and gloat, looking down—in every sense—on the little people who had made him rich.

I waited a long time for McMillin's ghost to show up in that head chair. The snow fell through the opening above and piled up on the chairs and table and floor—but nothing else happened.

Standing quietly by my side, Charlotte fixed a grown-up, worried look on me, and I realized I was waiting for nothing. The snow would fall, then it would stop falling, and the spring would come, but no McMillin would ever appear to hear me out. He wasn't there. All that was left was his ashes, and his chair, and this weird memorial.

Then I thought, I could sit in that chair myself. McMillin's chair. I could survey the land with his eyes, the eyes of a man who owns everything he sees. There was no one to stop me. No one to tell me it wasn't my place, that I wasn't good enough.

But I didn't want to. And I suddenly realized, that was what I'd come for. Not to see old buildings, or new ones, or the remembered outline of a harbor and out-lying islands. But to know I didn't want to be McMillin—not him or anyone like him. I never had and never would. The last of my anger fell away, and I was free.

"I'm done here, Charlotte," I told her. "We can go now."

I knew now how to get somewhere just by wishing. Holding Charlotte's hand, I wished us to wherever we were supposed to be.

12

We stood on a quiet street in Friday Harbor at dusk, outside a plain little house with a car in the driveway. Nothing seemed to be happening. There were no cars passing, no people walking, nothing but lighted windows and snow falling all around. Then I heard footsteps crunching on the sidewalk drifts, and I turned to see the homeless man coming our way.

"Good evening," he said, stopping beside us.

I returned his greeting nervously. I had no idea why he was there. For a while, the three of us stood silently outside the little house. Then the door opened, and the old woman we'd seen at the cemetery came out.

"There you are!" she said to the homeless man. He nodded.

She turned to us. "I remember you. I saw you at the cemetery a while ago."

Surprised, I turned to the homeless man. "I told you some people could see you," he reminded me. Then he asked the woman, "Are you ready?"

"I do wish it weren't just before Christmas. The family will be upset."

"It happens," he said.

She nodded and handed him her keys. "We have to hurry, or we'll miss the last ferry."

"We won't miss this one," he told her. "It will wait."

He opened the passenger door of the car to let her in, then gently closed it behind her. Then he turned back to Charlotte and me.

"Are you coming?"

"Where?"

Instead of answering, he vanished. More than vanished—he turned into a door, an open door. I looked through him and saw Mattie and me standing in front of a preacher, saying our marriage vows. There were only a few guests, but I knew one of the women in the background was my mother.

I blinked, and the scene changed. A man sat at a desk, unloading a pistol. He put the bullets neatly back in their box, then returned the gun to the back of his desk drawer and closed it.

As he leaned back with a look of relief, a girl in a pink dress burst into the room with her mother behind, both of them fresh from a children's party. He hugged them, and I knew what he was thinking: *I have to tell them I've lost the store, that we're broke. But we'll go on together. I must have been crazy for a few minutes there. Thank God I came to my senses. Nothing's that desperate. Nothing.*

Then I saw one more scene—Mattie and I, a little older, making a fuss over our own daughter. She looked like every little girl ever in the world, as if they'd somehow *all* been my daughter. She looked a lot like Charlotte.

I blinked again, and the homeless man stood there, waiting. I knew what he'd shown me—the door of heaven. All the things I'd seen were as real as the past we'd lived, and they were waiting for us.

"Are you coming?" he asked again.

I looked at Charlotte and saw that she had seen it all, too. Still holding hands, we scrambled into the backseat, and the homeless man backed us out of the driveway.

None of us spoke as he drove us down to the dock. A boat slid quietly across the dark water to receive us.

And we left the island.

ANNE L. WATSON, a retired historic preservation architecture consultant, is the author of numerous novels, plus books on such diverse subjects as soapmaking and baking with cookie molds. She currently lives in Friday Harbor, Washington, in the San Juan Islands—the setting of *Departure*—with her husband and fellow author, Aaron Shepard. Please visit her at **www.annelwatson.com**.